The Bugman Is After Me!

"I heard about some kids who cut across the Bugman's lawn once—and a whole swarm of wasps went after them," Carl told me. "They got about a million stings each. And cracking his tombstone is a lot worse than walking on his lawn."

"Even if that story is true—and it isn't—the Bugman is dead now," I told him. "He's been dead for a long time."

"Yeah, you're right," Carl said. "I guess he can't do anything to you."

"I'm going in to get something to drink," I announced. I stood up. Expecting Carl to tag along—as usual.

But he didn't move. He stared up at me. His mouth hanging open. His gray eyes bulging. Not a pretty sight.

"What?" I asked.

"Freeze," he whispered. "It's starting."

Carl sounded scared. I felt my stomach twist. *"What?"*

Carl slowly pushed himself to his feet. "There is a giant wasp crawling on your shoulder. It has to be one of *his.*"

Also from R. L. Stine:

The Beast
The Beast 2

Available from MINSTREL Books

THE
BUGMAN LIVES!

A Parachute Press Book

A
MINSTREL®
BOOK

PUBLISHED BY POCKET BOOKS

New York   London   Toronto   Sydney   Tokyo   Singapore

A MINSTREL PAPERBACK *Original*

 A Minstrel Paperback published by
POCKET BOOKS, a division of Simon & Schuster Inc.
1230 Avenue of the Americas, New York, NY 10020

ISBN: 0-671-52950-1

First Minstrel Books printing July 1996

10 9 8 7 6 5 4 3 2 1

THE
BUGMAN LIVES!

1

"Hey, Janet! Want to see me jump the curb?" Carl Beemer *whooshed* past me on his Rollerblades.

I didn't look up from my weeding. I didn't want to watch Carl jump the curb. I didn't want to watch him do anything—except skate away.

Carl is a pain. All he does is brag, brag, brag.

Carl zoomed up the front walk and stopped next to me. "Having fun?" he taunted.

Ignore him, I told myself. Maybe he'll leave. I kept working on the flower bed. Jabbing at the dirt and pulling out the weeds.

"I bet you aren't getting paid for that, are you?" Carl asked.

I wasn't. Mom says weeding is part of my family responsibilities. But Carl didn't have to know that. "None of your business," I muttered.

Carl laughed. "You aren't," he guessed.

I felt my face get hot. I hate it when Carl is right.

Carl stuck one of his big feet in front of me. "See my new Rollerblades? Cool, huh? I paid for them myself. I'm making big bucks with my mowing business."

I sat back in the grass and stared up at him. "Really? Maybe I'll get some jobs, too." If Carl could make money mowing lawns, I knew I could. I can do anything Carl can do—except better.

"Yeah, right," Carl answered. "Who would hire you?"

"Lots of people," I shot back. "By the end of the week I'll have more jobs than you do."

"No way!" Carl protested.

"Remember the recycling contest at school?" I asked. "I brought in eighteen more pounds of paper than you did."

Carl snorted. He sounds like a hog when he does that. "If I knew old telephone books counted, I would have beat you."

"Janet," Mom called from the house. "Are you getting those flower beds weeded?"

2

"Almost done!" I yelled back.

Carl snickered. "Yeah, Janet. Just think of all the money you're making doing that weeding." He skated off.

I rocked forward onto my knees again and started yanking up the weeds as fast as I could. I had to find some mowing jobs right away. I wanted *twice* as many as Carl had.

If I earned enough money, maybe I could go to camp next year like my friends. Then I wouldn't have to spend another summer in Shadyside with only Carl Beemer for company.

I scooped up all the weeds and stuffed them in a big plastic bag. "Mom!" I yelled. "I'm done. I'm going for a walk, okay?"

"See you later," she called.

I rushed over to our next-door neighbor's house. I combed my short, curly brown hair with my fingers and brushed the dirt off my shorts. Then I rang the bell.

Mrs. Kemp opened the door and peered at me through the screen.

"Hi, Mrs. Kemp," I said. "Do you need someone to mow your lawn this summer? I'm a good mower."

Mrs. Kemp smiled. "Sorry, Janet. I have a lawn service that does all my yard work."

"Oh," I said, feeling disappointed. "Well, thanks

3

anyway." I hurried back to the sidewalk. At least Carl didn't see that, I thought.

Then I heard him laughing. Carl popped out from behind the big oak tree in Mrs. Kemp's yard. "I'm a good mower," he squeaked in a high little voice.

"I don't sound like that!" I exclaimed.

"I don't sound like that!" Carl squeaked.

I stomped over to the next house. I heard the *shoop shoop* of Carl's skates behind me.

Why isn't Carl at camp this summer like Anita and Sara? I thought. Or at the Grand Canyon with his family like my best friend, Megan? Or visiting his grandmother like Toad?

Why does he have to be the one kid in the neighborhood—besides me—who is stuck spending the summer in Shadyside?

I rushed up to the Hoffmans' door. They didn't need their lawn mowed, either. And neither did the Hasslers, the Martins, or the Prescotts.

But I refused to give up. Especially with Carl watching.

I trooped through the neighborhood trying every house. Everyone told me they mowed their own lawn or they had already hired someone.

One guy had already hired *Carl.* Of course, Carl didn't bother to tell me that before I went to the door and asked. The jerk.

"You're striking out big time," Carl informed me. "You can't get a job anywhere!"

It took all my strength to keep from turning around and knocking his head off. "Why do you keep following me?" I demanded. "Go away. Get a life."

But he stayed right behind me. Of course. Carl never did anything I wanted him to.

I turned the corner—and heard Carl give a big gasp.

"*Ooooo*—Fear Street!" he teased. I glanced back at him. He had both his hands stuffed in his mouth, pretending to bite off all his fingernails.

Carl thinks he is hilarious. I shook my head as I started toward the first house.

This place definitely needs my help, I thought. High grass covered most of the crooked stone walkway. Weeds were taking over the flower beds. And dark green ivy clung to the porch railing and the front of the house.

I climbed the porch steps and rang the bell. A woman about my mom's age opened the door. She had short black hair, and she looked friendly.

"Hi," I said. "My name is Janet Monroe. I wondered if you need someone to mow your lawn this summer."

She smiled. I noticed she had a little gap between

her top two teeth. "That would be wonderful. I've been looking in the paper for someone to help me with the yard. Your timing is perfect."

"Fantastic!" I exclaimed.

"I'm Iris Lowy," the woman said. "When can you start, Janet? As you can see, my yard needs a *lot* of work." We both laughed.

"I can start right now," I told her.

"Great. How much do you charge?"

"Umm, four-fifty an hour," I said. I hoped that was okay. I hadn't thought about how much to ask for.

"Sounds fair," Mrs. Lowy answered. "The lawn mower is in the garage." She pointed around to the side of the house.

"Thanks," I said. As soon as she closed the door, I turned and grinned at Carl.

"So you got one lousy job," Carl taunted. "Big deal." He skated off down the street.

Finally, I thought. At least he isn't hanging around to watch me work.

I trotted up to the garage and wheeled out the mower. An old gas one. The kind you have to start by pulling a cord.

I hauled it through a wooden gate and into the side yard. I sighed as I gazed at the long strip of overgrown grass.

You wanted a job, I reminded myself. I yanked on the pull cord. Nothing.

I gave the cord another yank. Nothing.

"Come on, come on," I muttered.

I jerked the cord again. The motor blasted into action. The vibration raced up my hands and through my body.

I leaned my weight into the mower and pushed. I could feel the muscles in the backs of my legs strain as I struggled across the side yard.

The air was so heavy and hot I could hardly breathe. Sweat slid down my back. It trickled down my forehead and dripped into my eyes.

I knew Carl would love it if I quit, so I pictured him watching me with a stupid grin on his face. That helped me keep mowing.

My palms burned and itched against the handle of the mower. By the time I finished the side yard, I could feel blisters forming on both of them. And my hands are pretty tough.

I stopped the mower, letting the engine idle. I wiped my face on my sleeve and took in a deep breath. I love the smell of freshly cut grass.

I shook my arms out at my sides. My muscles already felt sore—and I had barely started.

I rolled the mower around to the backyard.

That's when I saw it.

A huge, tangled mass of tall weeds and grass in the far corner of the yard.

The rectangle-shaped patch wasn't that big—it looked about the size of the rug we have in our front hallway. But some of the weeds grew higher than my waist.

I should get it over with, I decided. I dragged the mower over to the patch.

Hundreds of tiny black bugs buzzed in the grass. And some of the weeds looked really prickly.

You can do it, I told myself. I aimed the mower at the patch and shoved as hard as I could.

The grass tangled around my knees. Thistles scratched my legs. I could feel the little bugs crawling over my bare skin.

Wheer! The mower squealed as I forced it through the patch. My muscles trembled with the effort.

The scream of the mower grew louder and louder. I didn't think I could stand another second of it. I wanted to cover my ears.

I slammed myself against the mower. Giving it one last huge shove.

Crack!

The mower bashed into something.

The motor groaned to a stop.

What happened? What made that horrible cracking sound?

I pulled the mower back and crouched down. I

8

shoved the grass back with my hands and found a stone.

A large, flat stone.

I ran my fingers over it. It felt icy cold. And smooth.

Then I felt deep grooves. I pushed more grass out of the way. And I saw the word HERE chiseled into the stone.

I yanked away clumps of weeds with both hands until I uncovered the whole stone.

It was one of the hottest days of the summer—but a cold shiver ran up my back when I read the words carved there.

HERE LIES THE BUGMAN. WOE TO ANYONE WHO WAKES HIM.

2

I jumped up.

A tombstone? I thought. Someone is *buried* under there. I'm standing on a grave.

I backed away. My feet got tangled in the weeds and I hit the ground hard.

I could feel weeds poking into my back. A swarm of tiny black gnats hovered above my face.

I'm on a grave, I thought.

I fell right on top of a grave. My heart thudded. I scrambled to my feet. And looked down.

HERE LIES THE BUGMAN. WOE TO ANYONE WHO WAKES HIM.

Right through the stone was a big jagged crack. A crack I made.

I turned and ran to Mrs. Lowy's back door. I pounded on it.

Mrs. Lowy jerked the door open. "Janet, what happened?" she asked. "Are you hurt?"

"I think I ran over a tombstone with the mower and broke it," I said. All my words ran together.

"What?" Mrs. Lowy cried. "A tombstone?"

I pulled in a deep breath and tried to talk more slowly. "I was mowing that overgrown patch in the side over there and I hit something. I think it's a tombstone."

"It can't be," Mrs. Lowy said. "Show me."

"Okay." I led the way back over to the stone and pointed down at it. My hand was shaking.

"My, my," Mrs. Lowy said. "I would have been scared if I found that, too. But it has to be a joke. Some teenagers probably heard those old stories about the Bugman and thought it would be funny."

"What stories?" I asked.

"Oh, you know. Stories about the man who used to live in the house next door years and years ago," she told me.

I shook my head. I still didn't know what she was talking about.

"Everyone called him the Bugman. He was fascinated by bugs and spent all his time studying them,"

Mrs. Lowy continued. "He was odd—didn't go out much or talk to his neighbors. People said he eventually turned into a bug himself."

"That's creepy." I wrapped my arms tightly around myself.

"Well, you know how everyone likes to tell stories about Fear Street," Mrs. Lowy said. "I'm sure someone put that stone there as a prank. I've never seen it before. And I've lived here for five years."

I nodded and tried to smile. I didn't want Mrs. Lowy to think I was a baby.

"Don't bother to finish that spot," Mrs. Lowy said. "It's not part of my yard anyway. It belongs to the house next door. Whoever ends up buying the house can deal with it."

"You mean no one lives there?" I glanced over at the other house. It was in worse shape than Mrs. Lowy's.

"It's been empty for years. I wish someone would take it. It would be nice to have neighbors." Mrs. Lowy sighed. "Do you want a Coke or anything before you go back to work?" she asked.

"No, thanks," I told her. I wanted to get out of there—fast.

"If you change your mind, let me know," Mrs. Lowy called as she headed back to the house.

I grabbed the mower handle. I ignored the blisters

on my hands, my sore arms and legs, and the heat. All I cared about was finishing the job so I could leave. I turned the mower around and went back to work.

But I couldn't stop thinking about the tombstone. The word *Bugman* pounded in my head with every step.

Bugman.

Bugman.

Bugman.

"Come on, Janet," I said to myself. "Chill out." I decided to check the tombstone. Maybe it wasn't as bad as I thought.

I left the mower running and rushed over to the stone. The huge crack was still there. The stone was split in half.

I read the words again. HERE LIES THE BUGMAN. WOE TO ANYONE WHO WAKES HIM.

What if I did wake him? What if he climbed out of his grave? What if he's watching me right now? What if—

Stop it, I ordered myself. I marched back over to the mower. Mrs. Lowy is right. The tombstone is just a stupid joke.

I glanced at it over my shoulder. Nothing.

I pushed the mower a little farther. Then I looked back at the tombstone again. Nothing.

It's going to take all day if I keep stopping to make sure the Bugman isn't coming out of his tomb! I thought.

"So you finally finished," Carl called. "Took you long enough." He jumped out of the cedar tree in my front yard and landed right in front of me.

I groaned. "Carl, don't you have a home?"

"Mowing is hard work. I bet you're ready to quit. If they want you to do the lawn again, you can give them my number," Carl volunteered.

"No way!" I plopped down on the grass and picked off some of the thistles stuck to my shorts. "Mrs. Lowy already hired me for the rest of the summer. She wants me to weed and water, too."

Carl sat down with his back against the tree trunk. "How did you get all those little cuts?"

Talking to Carl is better than talking to nobody, I decided. A little better.

"One spot in the backyard had all this high grass and weeds and thistles," I answered. "Something weird happened when I started mowing it. I ran into a big stone—"

"That was stupid," Carl said. "You could have busted the mower."

I ignored him. "It looked like a tombstone. It had words carved on it—'Here Lies the Bugman. Woe to

Anyone Who Wakes Him.' And I cracked it right down the middle."

"So?" Carl said, trying to sound bored.

"Mrs. Lowy—the lady who hired me—said this guy called the Bugman lived in the house next door to her more than fifty years ago," I explained. "He studied bugs—and some people thought he was turning into one."

"And you cracked open his tombstone?" Carl asked. "Aren't you scared? The tombstone said 'Woe to anyone who wakes him.' That means you."

Carl sounded happy. "Woe! Woe! Woe! Woe!" he chanted.

Why do I bother talking to him? "Mrs. Lowy thinks some kids put the tombstone there as a joke," I said.

"And you believed her?" Carl asked. "Adults always tell kids stuff like that. She probably didn't want you to get scared."

"I wasn't scared," I said quickly. "It's just an old story." No way was I admitting the truth to Carl.

"You should be scared," Carl warned. "I've heard of the Bugman. My uncle Rich told me about him. He could control insects. He could make them do anything he wanted. Sting people. Or spy on them and report back. Or—"

"Oh, right," I snapped. I studied Carl's face. He could be making the whole thing up to torture me.

Or he could be telling the truth.

"Really," Carl insisted. "I heard about some kids who cut across his lawn once—and a whole swarm of wasps went after them. They got about a million stings each. And cracking his tombstone is a lot worse than walking on his lawn."

"Even if that story is true—and it isn't—the Bugman is dead now," I told him. "He's been dead for a long time."

"Yeah, you're right," Carl said. "I guess he can't do anything to you."

"I'm going in to get something to drink," I announced. I stood up. Expecting Carl to tag along—as usual.

But he didn't move. He stared up at me. His mouth hanging open. His gray eyes bulging. Not a pretty sight.

"What?" I asked.

"Freeze," he whispered. "It's starting."

Carl sounded scared. I felt my stomach twist. *"What?"*

Carl slowly pushed himself to his feet. "There is a giant wasp crawling on your shoulder. It has to be one of *his*. The Bugman is after you."

3

"Don't move," Carl said in a low voice, creeping closer.

"Just get it off," I whispered. I didn't know how much longer I could stand still.

"It's crawling around your back now," he whispered. "Hold it, hold it. Don't move. There!"

Whap! Carl smacked his hand down on my back—hard!

"Ha, ha! You really fell for that one!" Carl cried. He cracked up. "Get it off! Get it off!" he squeaked in that high little voice that is supposed to sound like mine.

I hate Carl. I really, really hate him.

"You jerk!" I shouted. I gave him a hard punch on the shoulder. Then I stalked into the house and slammed the door behind me.

Carl made up that whole stupid story, I reminded myself when I rode up to Mrs. Lowy's house two days later. And that tombstone is a fake. Just a dumb joke.

I parked my bike in the side yard and hurried into the garage to get gardening tools. Mrs. Lowy wasn't home—but I found the tools right where she said I would. Good.

I'll start with that bed of red and white flowers near the big tree in the front yard, I decided. I ambled over and sat down in the shade. Then I pulled on a pair of gardening gloves—I wanted to protect my hands. I had tons of blisters from all the mowing.

Weeding for money is a lot more fun than weeding for free, I thought as I worked. And in the front yard I didn't have to look at the tombstone.

My eyes wandered over to the old reddish-brown house next door. The paint was flaking off in spots, exposing a coat of dingy white paint underneath. It reminded me of somebody's skin peeling after a bad sunburn.

I turned back to the weeding. How did all the stories about the Bugman get started? I wondered.

I yanked up weed after weed. Maybe the Bugman was a scientist, I thought. That's why he spent all his time with bugs.

Or maybe his name was something like Buckman—and some little kid misunderstood it. That could have started all the weird stories. I gathered up a bunch of the weeds and stuffed them in a garbage bag.

My body felt sore all over. I pulled off my gloves and stood up. I stretched my arms over my head as high as I could, going all the way up on my toes.

Wait. I spotted someone in one of the upper-story windows next door. Someone staring down at me.

I dropped back down on my heels. Is someone in that house? It's supposed to be empty.

A drop of sweat rolled into one of my eyes. I wiped my face with the hem of my T-shirt and stared back at the house.

The curtain in the window fluttered.

I kept watching. Waiting.

No movement. Nothing.

I must have imagined it.

Back to work, I thought. I wiped my face again. Then plopped back down on the grass and pulled on one of the gardening gloves.

"Oww!" I shouted. Something jabbed into my finger. I yanked off the glove.

A bee! I got stung by a bee! It must have crawled inside the glove.

My finger was already red and swollen.

I jumped to my feet, shaking my hand back and forth. Trying to cool off my stinging finger.

I should run it under the hose, I thought. I dashed toward the garage—and tripped on the stone walkway.

"Are you hurt?" someone asked.

I looked up. A man loomed over me. He leaned down and peered at me through his thick, thick glasses. His eyes were huge. The biggest eyes I ever saw.

The hair on my arms stood up. The man's unblinking black eyes gave me the creeps.

"Are you all right?" he asked in a thin, high voice. "I heard you yell, then I saw you fall."

"I got a bee sting on my finger," I explained. "I was running over to the hose and I tripped."

He held out his hand. It was long and thin, and covered by a brown work glove.

I pretended I didn't notice it and stood up. The pain in my sore finger was killing me.

"Come on. I'll get you some ice," he said.

Ice would feel great on the sting. "Thanks," I answered.

He led the way across the lawn. I slowed down when I realized where he was headed. The old deserted house next door. I *did* see someone over there, I thought.

The man glanced at me curiously, so I sped up again. I shot a quick look at him. He must be hot in all those clothes. He wore a baggy long-sleeved black shirt buttoned all the way to the top, long green pants, and a floppy brown hat.

Not one speck of skin showed. Except for his face.

Weird, I thought. I stopped in the front of the porch. "Um, Mrs. Lowy told me no one lived here," I said.

"I just moved in yesterday," he answered. "I'm Mr. Cooney and I'm renting the house for the summer. I'll be right back with the ice. Sit down." He gestured to a couple of wicker chairs on the porch.

"Thanks." I could hear him humming to himself as he disappeared through the screen door. I peered after him, but I couldn't see inside the house.

A few minutes later Mr. Cooney came back out the screen door. He carried a tray with a pitcher, two glasses, and a little plastic bag full of ice.

He set the tray down and handed me the ice. "That should take the sting out," he said.

I pressed the ice against my finger. The skin started getting numb right away.

"Would you like some juice?" he asked. He held up a pitcher filled with green liquid.

"What kind is it?" I asked.

"Oh, it's a mixture of fresh fruits. I'm a health-food nut."

"Okay, great," I said.

He picked up a glass and filled it almost to the top. He handed it to me, then poured a glass for himself.

"Oh, my name's Janet Monroe," I told him. I set the juice on the porch rail so I could hold the ice on my finger.

"Do you live next door?" he asked, then took a long gulp of his juice.

"No. I don't live on Fear Street. The lady who lives here hired me to do yard work," I explained.

He gazed at me through his thick glasses. "This house is quite run down, as you can see," Mr. Cooney said. "The yard needs a lot of attention. Would you be interested in doing some work for me, too?"

"That would be great!" I exclaimed. I couldn't wait to tell Carl. He's going to be sorry he gave me the idea of doing yard work, I thought. Between this place and Mrs. Lowy's, I'll be making a ton of money.

Mr. Cooney smiled. "Drink your juice," he urged.

"It looks strange, but it tastes good. You can get dehydrated working in the sun all day."

I was thirsty. I set down the ice and picked up the glass. I tilted my head back, closed my eyes, and gulped down the juice.

The cold, sweet liquid felt so good.

I opened my eyes. Something brushed against my top lip, something was going into my mouth. Something prickly. I crossed my eyes, trying to see what it was.

Something dark. Something shiny.

Something alive.

4

Gross!

My stomach lurched. I spit the rest of the juice over the porch railing.

"A *beetle!*" I shrieked. "There's a beetle in my juice! And it's alive!"

Coughing and choking, I stared into the glass at the huge bug. Its wings dripped with the sticky green juice.

I dropped the glass and scrubbed my mouth with my fingers. Hard. I couldn't get the feel of that disgusting beetle off my lips.

I squeezed past Mr. Cooney. I spotted a hose near

the side of the house and raced over to it. Then I turned it on full blast.

I took a huge gulp of water. I swished it around in my mouth and spit. If I didn't get rid of that horrible feeling, I would be sick right there.

"Sorry," Mr. Cooney called from the porch. "It must have fallen in the pitcher."

I went back to the porch, picked up the glass, and reached out to drop the beetle on the ground.

"Don't!" Mr. Cooney screeched. His eyes glistened behind his glasses.

I stopped, startled.

"I'll take care of it," he continued more softly.

I handed him the glass. He carefully fished the beetle out and put it on the porch railing.

Mr. Cooney set the glass on the porch railing, too. "So, Janet, when can you start work?" he asked.

"Is tomorrow okay?" I wanted to go to the town pool after I finished Mrs. Lowy's weeding.

"Sure," he answered. "See you then."

I rode my bike straight from Mrs. Lowy's to the pool. I spread some sunscreen on my arms and legs. Then I stretched out on my big black and white beach towel. The one I got free for being the first caller to answer KLIV's music trivia question.

Some little kids splashed around in the wading pool. A few seventh graders I recognized took turns on the high dive. And a couple of guys stood around talking to the teenage girl on lifeguard duty. But I couldn't find one person I knew to hang out with.

I wish Megan would hurry up and get back from vacation, I thought. It's not that fun spending the afternoon at the pool with no one to talk to.

Oh, well. It's a lot better than weeding and mowing, I reminded myself. I closed my eyes. Enjoying the hot sun on my skin.

I like to wait until I can't stand being in the sun one more second. Then I jump right into the deep end. The cold water feels great.

Whap!

"Ow!" My stomach stung like crazy.

I didn't even have to open my eyes to know what happened. "You're dead, Carl!" I yelled. I sat up and grabbed his towel away before he could snap me with it again.

Carl laughed. "I'm sooo scared," he answered. Then he cannonballed into the pool.

Whoosh! The giant wave Carl created drenched me. "Jerk," I muttered.

Carl came up for air. Still laughing.

I leaned over and splashed water into his face until he started to choke. The lifeguard gave me a dirty look—so I stopped.

Carl hoisted himself out of the pool and plopped down next to me.

"I got another mowing job," I announced before he could say a word.

"Two jobs. Big deal." Carl snorted.

"Yeah, but my new job is huge. I'll be working tons—a lot more than you," I told him.

"Where is this *huge* job?" Carl demanded.

I hesitated. "Next door to Mrs. Lowy," I said.

"The *Bugman's* house?" Carl yelled. "You're working for the Bugman?"

"I'm not working for the Bugman," I protested. "I'm working for Mr. Cooney. He lives in the house where the Bugman *used* to live. The Bugman is dead—get it?"

"Big mistake," Carl said. He pointed to my leg. "Look! He sent another one of his bug friends after you."

My heart give a hard *thump*.

I felt tiny legs traveling toward my knee.

I didn't want to look. But I forced myself to glance down.

A ladybug. That's all. A little red and black ladybug crawling up my leg.

I reached down to flick it off.

"Noooooo!" someone screamed.

5

〜

"**D**on't do that! You'll be sorry." A girl in a purple and yellow bathing suit ran toward me. "Noooo!" she screamed. "Don't do it. Leave that ladybug alone. It's bad luck."

The girl threw herself down next to me. She stuck her finger in front of the ladybug—and it crawled right on. "Poor baby," she crooned.

Carl snorted.

I didn't even glance at him. This strange girl was talking to a bug.

She looked up at me. "Sorry if I scared you by

yelling like that," the girl apologized. "But I couldn't let you hurt this little ladybug."

"It's a bug," Carl said loudly. "A stupid bug. What's your problem?"

"Every creature on earth deserves life," she told us. "That's what my whole family believes. We don't eat meat or fish or eggs. Even our cat is a vegetarian."

"Sorry," I mumbled. "I wasn't really trying to kill it. I just wanted it off me."

The girl nodded. "Most people don't ever think about bugs," she said. "If they did, they would probably treat them better."

The ladybug flew off the girl's finger. She gave it a little wave.

"What about spiders?" Carl demanded. "Or centipedes? I bet you kill them."

"I don't believe in murder," the girl answered. "When you kill anything—even a spider—you upset the balance of the universe."

Carl snorted again.

"Did you know you sound like a pig when you do that?" the girl asked.

I laughed. That's exactly what I think every time Carl gives one of his snorts.

She's cool, I decided. Weird—but cool, too. And she has to be more fun than Carl.

"I'm Janet," I told the girl. "And he's Carl."

"I'm Willow," the girl said.

"What grade are you in?" I asked. "I've never seen you at school."

"I'm going into sixth," Willow answered. "But I do home study. My family believes you can learn everything you need to know from the world around you."

Carl slid up to the edge of the pool and dangled his feet in the water. Ignoring us.

"So your parents teach you? Isn't that—" I began.

"Look!" Carl exclaimed. "There's an ant in the water. It's going to drown."

Willow scrambled next to Carl. "Where?"

"Right there!" he cried. "A big black one."

Willow leaned forward—and Carl started kicking as hard as he could. Splashing water into Willow's face.

"Carl, you idiot!" I yelled.

Willow jumped into the pool. She grabbed Carl by both feet and yanked him into the water.

Carl came up sputtering. He lunged for Willow. She twisted to the side—then dunked him again.

Definitely a cool girl, I thought.

"Say you're sorry!" Willow demanded.

"No way!" Carl choked out.

Dunk!

"Say it!" Willow ordered.

Carl shook his head. The stubborn expression on his face cracked me up.

Dunk!

"Okay, okay!" Carl shouted. "I'm *soooo* sorry. Are you happy now?"

"Yes," Willow told him calmly. She climbed out of the pool and sat down next to me.

"Why don't you take your new friend to the Bugman's house?" Carl urged me. "I bet they would get along great."

"Why don't you go see how long you can hold your breath under water?" I called back.

But Carl swung out of the pool and plopped himself down. He can't take a hint.

"Who's the Bugman?" Willow asked.

"He's a guy who loved bugs so much he turned into one," Carl told her. "So you better watch out. You could start growing extra legs any day." He gave Willow his best evil grin.

"Ignore him. It's just a dumb story," I protested.

The lifeguard blew her whistle. "Three o'clock," she announced. "Time for lap swimmers only. Everyone else out of the pool."

"I didn't know it was so late," Willow said. "I've got to go." She jumped up. "See you around," she called to me as she headed toward the locker room. "I come to the pool a lot."

Maybe this summer won't be so bad, I thought. I've got two jobs. And maybe I've found someone I can hang out with. Someone who *isn't* Carl.

I showed up at Mr. Cooney's early the next morning. I wanted to be done in time to go to the pool. I hoped Willow would be there again.

Mr. Cooney waved to me from the front porch. "I got the lawn mower out for you," he called. He pointed to a rusty mower by the porch steps.

I strolled over to it. No motor. Great, I thought. Just great.

"Do you want to borrow a long-sleeved shirt?" Mr. Cooney asked, peering down at me through those extra-thick glasses. "It isn't good for you to get too much sun, you know."

No way would Mr. Cooney ever get sunburned. He had on the same outfit as yesterday. Long pants, long-sleeved shirt buttoned all the way up, work gloves, and a hat.

Very strange guy. "No, thanks," I answered. I grabbed the mower handle. "My mom always makes me put on sunscreen."

"Okay." Mr. Cooney wandered back into the house. Humming to himself. Not a song. Just the same note over and over. *Hmm. Hmm. Hmm.*

I shook my head. He should get a Walkman, I thought.

I attacked the lawn. Pushing myself to mow as fast as I could.

By the time I finished, my T-shirt was glued to my back. I knew my face had to be bright red.

I checked my watch. Almost 2:10. If I hurried I could make it to the pool before 2:30.

But first I had to get paid.

I stared up at the big, old house. The curtains were drawn in every window. He must really hate the sun, I thought. I would hate to live in the dark that way.

I climbed up the porch steps. The heavy front door stood open beyond the screen. I knocked on the doorframe.

Quiet. No footsteps heading toward the door. Nothing.

I knocked again—harder.

He's got to be home, I thought. I know it. I would have noticed him leave.

I pressed my face against the screen door. But I still couldn't see anything. Too dark inside.

"Mr. Cooney?" I called. "I need to leave now!"

No answer.

I opened the door and stepped inside. The house smelled damp. Moldy.

My eyes adjusted to the dim room. A thick layer of dust covered everything—the warped wood floor, the flowered sofa, the green curtains. And there were no lamps anywhere.

This place is really creepy, I thought.

"Mr. Cooney?" I called again.

I walked down the hall.

Nothing. A door ahead of me was open a crack. I headed for it. All I wanted to do was get my money and get out of there.

I knocked on the door and it swung all the way open. I stepped inside.

There was Mr. Cooney, by a long table at the other end of the room. His back to me.

"How are you feeling today, hmm? You look well," he crooned in his high voice.

I stared around the dimly lit room. I didn't see anyone but Mr. Cooney.

"Yesss. Yesss. You are looking much better, my baby," he murmured. He turned slightly.

He raised his hand up in front of him.

Something sat there. Something black. Something hairy.

A tarantula!

Mr. Cooney brought the huge spider close to his lips.

Closer. Closer.

Then he did something that made me feel sick.

6

He kissed the spider!

How could he stand kissing a tarantula? How could he stand feeling that bristly black hair against his lips?

"I love you, my baby," Mr. Cooney cooed in his high voice. He kissed the giant spider again.

I gasped. I couldn't help it.

Mr. Cooney jerked his head toward me.

He strode across the room. The tarantula still in his hand.

I took a step backward—and bumped into the

doorjamb. "K-keep it away from me," I stammered. "Please."

Mr. Cooney stopped. "Oh!" he exclaimed. He returned to the table and set the tarantula down.

"I forget that everyone isn't as comfortable around spiders as I am," he apologized when he turned to face me again.

"Um, it's okay," I said in a rush. "I finished mowing the lawns. And . . . uh . . . I came to get paid."

I could hardly look at him. I'll just pretend I didn't see anything, I decided. What else could I do? Tell him what a cute spider he had? Yeah, right.

"That's fine," he answered. He didn't sound embarrassed or anything. He pulled out his wallet and handed me my pay. I put it in my pack. "Have a glass of juice before you go."

I nervously scanned the floor. Why does he have a tarantula? Does he have more than one of those spiders? I wanted out of there. Now.

"No, thanks," I blurted. "I—I have some water with me, and—"

"But your water must be warm by now," Mr. Cooney interrupted. He picked a pitcher up off the table and poured me a tall glass of the green juice.

He held the glass out to me. "Take it. It's a particularly good batch today."

I took the glass, checked it for bugs, then drank the juice in three big gulps.

I handed him the empty glass. "Thanks. I have to go. See you." I turned and rushed through the living room.

"I'll see you tomorrow," Mr. Cooney called as I slammed the screen door. Not if I see you first, I thought.

I jumped off the porch. I climbed on my bike and pedaled down the street as hard as I could.

Does he let that tarantula wander around his whole house? I wondered. I decided never to go inside again—just in case. Mr. Cooney could pay me out on the porch from now on.

He told that tarantula he loved it, I thought. That's so gross.

Suddenly I remembered what Mrs. Lowy told me about the Bugman. The Bugman loved bugs so much he started turning into one.

He *loved* bugs. And so did Mr. Cooney.

"Janet!" someone yelled.

I slowed down and glanced over my shoulder. Willow stood on the sidewalk.

I put on my brakes and jumped off the bike. "Didn't you hear me the first three times?" Willow complained.

"Sorry," I mumbled.

"Hey, what's wrong?" Willow asked. "You're all pale."

"It's sort of a long story," I told her. "Can you come over? I only live a couple blocks away."

"Sure," Willow answered. "I was heading over to the pool. But I can go later."

We started down the block. I walked my bike so we could talk. "You said you never heard of the Bugman, right?" I asked.

Willow nodded. Her green eyes serious.

"I hadn't, either. Until a couple days ago. . . ." I told her the whole story as we walked to my house.

Willow kicked a rock down the sidewalk. "You're giving me the creeps," she said when I got to the part about the Bugman turning into a bug. "You don't believe that story, do you?"

"No. And Mrs. Lowy said the tombstone had to be a joke. But here's the really weird part. Something really strange happened today."

We turned onto my front walk, and then I heard a familiar sound. *Shoop shoop. Shoop shoop.*

Great, I thought. All I need right now is Carl.

He zoomed past on his Rollerblades, then spun to a stop in front of us. "So what are we doing today?"

"What do you mean *we?*" I asked.

He acted as if he hadn't heard me. "You got any cookies?" He plopped down on the front porch and pulled off his skates.

"No. Go away." I rolled my eyes at Willow. She rolled her eyes back at me.

"Chips are okay then," Carl said. He stood up and walked into my house. Heading straight for the kitchen.

"Where did you find Junk Food Boy?" Willow whispered as we followed him.

"His mom and my mom are best friends," I explained. "I've known him since preschool. And I still haven't figured out how to get rid of him."

"Is that you, Janet?" my mother called from upstairs.

"Yeah!" I shouted back. "I brought a friend home. And Carl."

Willow giggled. "And Carl," she repeated.

"Make yourselves a snack," Mom answered.

Carl already had his head stuck in our refrigerator. "So how is the Bugman?" Carl asked. He slammed the fridge door shut and opened one of the cupboards.

I didn't answer. Willow and I sat down at the kitchen table. "Come on," she urged. "Tell me what happened."

Carl grabbed a bag of Fritos and ripped it open with his teeth. He sat down across from us and shoved a handful of the corn chips in his mouth. "Something happened?" he mumbled.

39

"Yeah." I turned to Willow. "Today when it was time to leave, I went inside to find Mr. Cooney."

I felt the back of my neck prickle. I was getting the creeps just thinking about what happened.

"I heard him talking to someone, but no one else was in the room." I glanced back and forth between Willow and Carl. "You won't believe what he was talking to," I continued.

The prickly feeling moved up the back of my head.

"A tarantula!" Carl cried.

"How did you know?" I demanded.

My ear started to itch. I reached up to scratch it.

"Don't!" Carl hollered.

"I'm not falling for that stupid joke again," I snapped.

"It's not a joke," Willow said quietly.

Something soft touched my cheek.

Then I caught sight of something black. Something long, and black, and hairy. Walking across my face.

7

A tarantula. A tarantula was on my face, walking onto my eyebrow.

I squeezed my eyes shut.

"Hold still," Carl said. He picked up the newspaper from the kitchen table. "I'm going to knock it off you."

"No!" Willow exclaimed. "I'll get something to put it in."

She raced over and threw open the cabinet doors—one after the other. "Don't be afraid," she called. "It won't bite you unless you scare it. And they aren't poisonous. Well, not poisonous enough to kill you."

The tarantula stepped onto my nose. Its bushy hair tickled my left nostril.

I heard Willow run back over to me. "You're okay," she said soothingly. "It's more afraid of you than you are of it."

I opened my eyes. Willow smiled in encouragement. She pressed a Tupperware container against my cheek. The she nudged the tarantula inside.

Whew!

"Put on the lid!" Carl ordered.

Willow held the lid against the container. "I can't seal it," she said. "The tarantula needs air."

I started to shake.

"It's all over," Willow said. "I'm going to make you a health shake. It will help you calm down," she added.

She picked up her purple and yellow backpack and hurried over to the kitchen counter.

I shoved my fingers through my hair. I scratched my scalp. I rubbed my face until my skin felt sore and hot. I brushed off my arms and legs.

But I kept feeling those spider legs crawling over me. Crawling everywhere. I stood up. "Carl, is there anything on my back?" I asked.

"No," he answered. His voice serious.

I studied the front of my shirt and arms and legs. Then I sat back down.

"Is it okay if I use your blender?" Willow asked.

"Yeah," I said. "There's fruit and stuff in the fridge."

"Whoa," Carl mumbled. He shook his head back and forth. "Whoa."

I stared down at the Tupperware container. I could see the tarantula moving around through the thick plastic.

Brraaap. Willow ran the blender at high speed.

A couple of minutes later she returned to the table with two thick, pale green shakes—and a Coke. She handed one of the shakes to me and the Coke to Carl. "Health shakes don't go with Fritos," she told him.

"Lucky for me," Carl answered.

"This is so weird," I muttered. "First I see a tarantula at Mr. Cooney's place. Then there's one here."

"It must have fallen into your backpack," Willow said.

"But that's not the weird part," I said. "Don't you think it's weird that a man who loves bugs would move into the Bugman's house?"

"There's only one thing that explains it," Carl said slowly.

"What?" I finally asked.

"Mr. Cooney *is* the Bugman," he answered.

"You moron," I snapped. "The Bugman is dead! That means Mr. Cooney cannot be the Bugman!"

"It's all the Fritos," Willow told me solemnly. "They're destroying his brain."

Carl shoved another handful of Fritos in his mouth. "I'm right," he mumbled. "You'll see."

The next day I fooled around as long as I could at Mrs. Lowy's. I watered the front and back lawn and did some trimming and weeding.

But I had to go over to Mr. Cooney's. He's not the Bugman, I told myself. The Bugman is dead— if there every really was a Bugman in the first place.

"Janet," Mr. Cooney called from the porch as soon as I started across his front lawn. "I got out the gardening tools for you."

I hope they're in better shape than his lawn mower, I thought. I hurried over and grabbed the tools off the porch railing.

"Have some juice before you start," Mr. Cooney said.

"No, thanks," I answered. "Mrs. Lowy just gave me a big glass of lemonade."

I turned toward the front flower bed. Mr. Cooney wasn't the Bugman. But that didn't mean I wanted to spend the morning sitting on the porch with him—especially after I saw him kiss that awful, ugly tarantula.

"I made this batch for *you*," Mr. Cooney said. I heard him climbing down the porch steps.

I sighed. Then I forced myself to smile as I turned back to him. "I'm really not thirsty," I said. "Thanks, anyway."

Mr. Cooney held a tall glass of the juice out toward me. "Drink it, Janet." His tone was sharp. And his wet black eyes gleamed behind the thick lenses of his glasses.

What is his problem? I wondered.

"Take it," he said again, his voice high and angry. "You must drink it."

No way am I drinking that stuff now, I thought. I took the glass from Mr. Cooney—and let it slip through my fingers. It shattered on the stone walkway.

"Oh, I'm so sorry!" I exclaimed. I hoped I sounded sincere.

"I'm such a klutz."

Mr. Cooney turned without a word. He marched back into the house.

He's furious at me, I thought. But I didn't care.

I bent down to pick up the pieces of broken glass.

Hundreds of tiny bugs came out of nowhere. They

surrounded the puddle of green juice. Hundreds. Thousands of bugs.

Sucking up the juice.

I kneeled down to get a closer look. As I watched, their bodies started to swell. To grow.

The bugs were doubling . . . no, tripling in size.

8

I stared down at the circle of insects.

What is going on here? I thought. What is in that juice? I drank that juice. *What is it doing to me?*

The screen door opened and slammed shut.

I saw Mr. Cooney rushing down the porch steps. Another big glass of the juice in his hand.

"Don't worry about spilling it," he said. "Plenty more where that came from."

I glanced down at the bugs again. They fought for the remaining juice. Their bodies still expanding.

A cricket swelled up. Growing rounder and rounder. Bigger and bigger. It sucked up more juice.

More juice—bigger and bigger.

Then *pop*. It exploded. Green goo spewed out everywhere. The other bugs swarmed around the cricket—and drank the liquid draining out of its body.

"Take the juice, Janet," Mr. Cooney whispered. "Take it."

"No!" I cried. "There's something horrible in that juice. I don't want it."

I turned and ran. Bugs crunching and squishing under my sneakers. Coating the bottoms with green slime.

"Janet!" Mr. Cooney yelled.

I didn't look back. I kept running. Running. Running.

The pool. I'll go to the pool. I'll relax. I'll think about what to do. Maybe Willow will show up. I can talk to her about this.

My side started to ache. I started to wheeze. But I didn't stop running until I reached the wire fence around the pool.

No Willow. Maybe she's in the locker room, I thought. I went over to the locker room.

I stared around. The locker room was almost empty. Just a mom trying to get her little girl to put on a pair of flip-flops.

Okay, I told myself. Calm down. You're safe now.

"What's wrong with her?" I heard the little girl ask. Her mother shushed her as they walked out.

I dropped down on one of the wooden benches and leaned forward. Trying to catch my breath.

That's when I saw it.

The scab on my knee. Shiny purple-black. About the size of a quarter—but thicker.

How did I get that? When did I hurt my knee?

I poked the scab with my finger. It felt hard. Hard and *crunchy*.

I jabbed the scab again. It cracked open . . . and oily green liquid oozed out.

Green liquid. Like Mr. Cooney's juice. My stomach lurched.

I closed my eyes and saw the cricket exploding again. Spraying green goo.

"No," I whispered. This can't have anything to do with the juice.

But it did. I knew it did.

I jumped up and rushed to the bathroom. I propped my knee up on one of the sinks and splashed it with hot water. As hot as I could stand.

Then I soaked a paper towel and covered it with the pink soap from the dispenser.

I scrubbed the scab. Scrubbed and scrubbed with the gritty soap. But it didn't come off.

The paper towel fell apart. I grabbed another one,

covered it with soap, and attacked the scab again. I had to get it off me. I had to.

This isn't working, I thought. I tossed the paper towel in the trash and started digging at the scab with my fingernails. Finally it popped off and fell into the sink.

I let my breath out with a *whoosh.* Then I ran hot water over my knee until the skin turned bright red and wrinkly.

I snapped off the water, eased my knee off the sink, and sat down on the tile floor.

I couldn't stop shivering.

Mr. Cooney's green juice did this to me, I thought. I know it. And that means . . . that means that Mr. Cooney could be the Bugman.

I slowly climbed to my feet.

I *knew* what I had to do.

I had to find out the truth about Mr. Cooney— and that green juice he kept feeding me.

I had to go back to his house.

After dark. It had to be after dark. I didn't want to get caught.

9

I stared across the dark street at Mr. Cooney's house. I'll have to get closer than this, I thought. A lot closer if I want to find out the truth about Mr. Cooney—and that disgusting green juice of his.

Okay, I decided. I'll count to three. Then I'll run over to the big pine tree in his front yard.

One. Two. Three.

I pounded across the street and pressed myself against the trunk of the tall tree. The bark felt rough against my cheek.

I peered around the tree trunk at the big old

house. No lights came on. I didn't hear footsteps or the sound of a door opening.

Safe. So far.

I wish Willow were here, I thought. Or even Carl.

But Willow never showed up at the pool. I didn't have her phone number or anything, so I couldn't tell her my plan.

And Carl was up in my room right now—playing tapes, eating cookies, and talking to himself. Mom and Dad thought I was up there with him. They would never suspect I slipped out while they sat watching TV.

Stop stalling, I ordered myself. Okay, now I'll count to three and climb the fence into the backyard.

I figured I'd have better luck in the back of the house. That's where I found Mr. Cooney kissing his tarantula.

One. Two. Three.

I dashed to the wooden fence and hauled myself to the top. Splinters dug into my palms. The fence groaned and creaked, shaking underneath me.

I jumped down into the backyard—and froze where I landed. Crouched down as low to the ground as possible.

Did he hear me?

I didn't move. My legs started to cramp. Worse than when our P.E. teacher Ms. Mason makes us do a million deep knee bends.

A dog barked, and I heard a guy yelling for it to shut up. Other than that, the neighborhood was still and quiet.

I circled around the house. Walking with my knees bent so I would be harder to see from the house. Almost there, I told myself. Almost there.

I pushed through the bushes that grew below the windows and strained to see inside. Too high. I stretched up onto my tiptoes—but still couldn't quite see inside. I needed something to stand on.

I glanced around the backyard. That plastic garbage can would probably work, I decided. I hope it's empty.

I squeezed back through the bushes and hurried over to the can. Good—empty. I pulled it underneath the window and flipped it over. Then I climbed on top.

The heavy plastic buckled under my weight. But the garbage can didn't collapse. Whew!

I rose up on my knees and peered into the window. I saw a big room glowing with a dim blue light.

I leaned into the room, bracing myself on the window ledge. Good thing Mr. Cooney loves bugs so much, I thought. I don't have to worry about window screens.

Tables filled the room. And on the tables stood row after row of huge glass tanks. That's where the light is coming from, I realized. The tanks.

I needed to see more. I had to go inside.

I took a deep breath and swung one leg into the room. The garbage can flew out from under me and landed with a *thud*.

He had to hear that, I thought. Should I run? No, I needed to keep going. I pulled my other leg inside and dropped to the floor.

I lifted my head—and stared straight into a tank of cockroaches. Their shiny brown bodies glistening as they climbed over a hunk of rotting meat.

I pushed myself to my feet and glanced down into the next tank. Centipedes. Thousands of them. I could hear a soft rustling sound as they crawled over one another, their antennae waving wildly. Gross.

The next tank held a brown and white rabbit. It stared up at me, its little pink nose twitching. What are you doing in here, little bunny? I thought.

The rabbit hopped toward its food bowl. And I saw the fat gray leech clinging to its stomach.

I squeezed my eyes shut for a moment. Then I opened them and forced myself to keep moving.

I felt as if I were in a maze. The tanks of insects forming hallways and corridors.

I was surrounded by bugs. Thousands and thousands of them. My skin started to itch. I could almost feel all those little legs scurrying over me.

I have to get out of here. Now, now, now. Looking at all these bugs isn't going to help me.

I wove through the rows of tanks. Rushing faster and faster. Trying to find my way to the door. Then I turned a sharp corner. What I saw made my heart give a hard thump against my rib cage.

Mr. Cooney sat hunched over an old-fashioned desk only a few feet from me. His back was turned, and he appeared absorbed in the papers in front of him.

I inched away from him. Quietly, so quietly. I didn't want to think about what he would do if he caught me spying on him.

I took a few more small steps back.

Mr. Cooney straightened up.

Did he hear me?

Mr. Cooney reached up toward the bookshelf over the desk.

Close, I thought. I glanced over at him again— and almost screamed.

Something was wrong with Mr. Cooney. Horribly wrong!

He didn't have a hand on the end of his arm.

He had a claw. An enormous claw. Sharp and gleaming.

Like the pincer of a giant bug!

10

Mr. Cooney stretched open his pincer and clamped down on a book.

He doesn't have hands. He's not human. Mr. Cooney is part bug!

It's the Bugman. Mr. Cooney *is* the Bugman!

I spun around—and slammed into one of the glass tanks.

I lunged for it. But I wasn't fast enough.

The tank crashed to the floor—exploding into a million shards of glass.

Tiny white maggots flew across the room. One hit

me in the forehead. It rolled down my cheek and dropped onto the floor.

"Babies!" Mr. Cooney shrieked. Then he saw me. "What have you done to my babies?"

I turned to face him. "I . . . I'm really, really sorry, Mr. Cooney. I didn't mean to. I just bumped into the tank, and, and . . ." I stammered. "I'll work it off, I promise."

"You think you can *pay* me, and my babies will be all right?" he screeched in fury. He pointed at the floor with his horrible pincer.

I stared down at the hundreds of maggots. Blindly crawling over the sharp glass.

"You hurt them!" Mr. Cooney exploded. He glared at me through his thick glasses. "Some of them might even be dead!"

"I'm sorry," I repeated. "I'm so, so sorry."

"Sorry," Mr. Cooney snarled. "Sorry." He stalked toward me, the broken glass crunching under his feet. "My babies are dead and you're *sorry?*"

Mr. Cooney reached up and tore off his thick glasses. Ragged pieces of skin pulled away with them. His nose fell onto the floor with a moist *plop!*

I screamed. Screamed until my throat felt raw.

Mr. Cooney grabbed a strip of skin from his forehead and yanked it away. He threw it down on the floor in front of my feet.

I clenched my teeth together to keep from screaming again. A low moan escaped my lips. I shook my head back and forth, back and forth.

He tore off his right ear. Ripped away his left. Oily green goo spattered across the floor.

Mr. Cooney gave a high squeal. He peeled away his lips.

A mask! His whole face is a mask, I realized.

Now I saw the real Mr. Cooney. The real *Bugman*.

He had the head of a giant fly. No nose. A sucker for a mouth. His skin covered with rough black bristles.

And his eyes. His eyes were the worst. They bulged away from his head. Wet and shiny.

They were divided into sections—like two enormous golf balls. I could see myself reflected over and over—in each part of his black eyes.

Mr. Cooney grabbed his floppy white hat and yanked it off. A long pair of antennas uncurled. One shot out and brushed against my cheek. It felt dry and rough.

Run, my mind ordered. Run!

But I couldn't. My legs wouldn't move. They felt rooted to the floor.

I couldn't look away from Mr. Cooney.

I heard a horrible moist sucking sound. I gazed around wildly. What is that?

I realized the sound came from Mr. Cooney's mouth.

He leaned closer toward me, his eyes glistening with anger.

And spat a stream of bright green liquid at me.

12

The green spit splattered across my bare arm. Bubbling and foaming until it soaked into my skin.

My skin turned dead white. And cold. Cold clear through to the bone. So cold it burned.

I heard Mr. Cooney making that sucking sound again. He's getting ready to spit! I realized.

I jumped back. I grabbed the closest tank and heaved it off the table. It shattered on the floor between me and Mr. Cooney. Pieces of glass flew across the room.

Hundreds of red ants poured out of the tank. The biggest ants I had ever seen.

Mr. Cooney shrieked in agony. He lunged toward me—his pincer clicking open and shut.

I dived under the nearest table—grinding the ants under my hands and knees. Their bites felt like hot needles jabbing into my skin, but I didn't stop. I couldn't stop.

I crawled out the other side and shoved the table over. Two more tanks crashed to the floor. I heard a furious buzzing, but I didn't look back to find out which insects I had released.

I dashed for the window. Stumbling as I followed the twists and turns of the maze of tanks.

I heard Mr. Cooney crooning to his *babies*. Then I heard him coming after me. His pincer snapping open and shut. *Click, click, click.*

I leaped for the windowsill and hauled myself on top. I wriggled through the opening on my stomach. I could see the backyard. See the grass and the trees and the lawn. Almost there. Almost there, I thought.

I pushed off with both hands—and something grabbed my foot. Squeezing it tighter and tighter. I twisted around and stared over my shoulder.

I saw Mr. Cooney's pincer locked around my ankle. "You're not going anywhere!" he shouted.

I kicked frantically. Tried to squirm away. Then I reached out of the window as far as I could and grabbed one of the bushes with both hands.

I pulled myself toward the bush. Fighting to hold on to the tiny branches.

Mr. Cooney yanked on my foot—hard. I almost lost my grip. He yanked again.

My shoe popped off in his pincer, and I fell face first into the bush.

I jumped up and ran. Raced around the house, over the fence, across the front lawn.

Is he following me? I didn't stop to check.

Tiny stones dug through my sock and into my foot. But I couldn't stop. Didn't stop until I reached my front door.

I pulled open the door and stumbled into the hallway. "Mom," I croaked. My throat too dry to yell. "Mom!" I tried again.

The room whirled around me. I felt dizzy, so dizzy. I couldn't stand up. I collapsed on the hard floor of the front hall.

My eyes drifted shut. I knew I should try to yell for help. But I felt too weak, too woozy.

I felt a cold hand on my forehead.

"Janet!" a voice called. It sounded so far away. "Janet, what's wrong?"

I forced my eyes halfway open. Mom!

"Is she okay?" someone else asked. I thought it was Carl.

"Mom," I mumbled. "Bugman's after me. He spit on me. I spilled his maggots . . . I mean his babies.

He likes to call them his babies. Didn't mean to, Mom."

My eyes fluttered shut again. I couldn't hold them open a moment longer.

"You're burning up," I heard Mom say. She sounded even farther away now. "You have a fever. But you're okay. . . . You're going to be okay. . . ."

I shook my head back and forth. I felt the floor rock beneath me. "No, no, no," I protested. "Don't understand. Don't understand, Mom. He pulled his *face* off. And he spit at me. And he's going to come after me."

"Herb!" Mom called in her teeny, tiny voice. Why did her voice sound so funny? "Herb, there's something wrong with Janet!"

I heard Dad running up. He touched my head with his big hand. "You're right. She's on fire."

"You go on home, Carl," Mom said. "I'll call your mother later."

"Dad," I begged. "You have to help me get away. The Bugman is coming. And he's so mad at me. I broke open his tombstone and then I hurt his babies. But I didn't mean to. I didn't mean to."

"It's like the time when she was six, remember?" Mom asked. I could hardly hear her. "She had a high fever and thought a man-eating plant was growing in her stomach."

"Let's get her to bed." I felt Dad scoop me up in his arms.

"I'm going to call the doctor," Mom answered.

All the colors in the room ran together, swirling around me. Swirling in front of my eyes. I couldn't see Mom and Dad anymore. But I knew Dad was carrying me up the stairs.

He put me down on the bed and pulled off my other shoe. The colors in front of my eyes faded. My head cleared a little.

That's when I saw it. On my arm. Right where the Bugman's spit landed.

A shiny purple-black scab about as big as my fist.

"No. No, no, no," I moaned.

I reached down and rubbed my fingers over the spot. It felt thick and hard. And *crunchy*.

Like the shell of a giant beetle.

13

"**D**ad, I'm turning into a bug. You've got to help me. Please." I struggled to sit up, but my dad pressed me back onto the bed.

"Shhh. Shhh," Dad coaxed. "You're safe, Janet. Nothing bad is going to happen to you. I'm right here."

I clawed at the big scab. I had to pull it off.

Dad caught both my hands in one of his. "Don't, Janet."

He doesn't understand, I thought. I have to make him understand.

I concentrated as hard as I could. Start at the

beginning, I thought. "Listen, please," I begged him. "I was mowing. *Mowing.* And I hit a tombstone—the Bugman's tombstone. And he's mad. He's so mad at me, Dad."

"No, no, Janet," Dad crooned. "He's not mad. Who could be mad at you?"

Mom rushed in and sat down on the bed next to me. I stared up at her. "Mom, I'm a bug. Dad doesn't understand. I'm a *bug.*"

"She's delirious," Dad said softly.

Mom slipped the thermometer under my tongue. "Don't talk now, Janet. We have to see how high your temperature is."

I opened my mouth to try and explain again. But my mom grabbed my chin lightly between her fingers. "You can't talk now. Keep still—only for a minute, okay?"

They're never going to believe me, I thought. Never.

"I called Dr. Walker," my mom told my dad. "She's out of town. I told her service it was an emergency, so the doctor who is covering for her is coming right over. He's supposed to be very good, too."

Doctor, I thought. Maybe a doctor could help me.

Mom pulled the thermometer out of my mouth. "A hundred and four," she said.

I lay still, focusing on what I needed to tell the doctor.

"Do you want some ice water, honey?" Mom asked.

I shook my head. I need to rest now, I thought. Rest so I can tell the doctor what the Bugman did to me. Maybe he can do tests on that green goo. That green goo in the scab.

I raised my arm and stared at the purple-black scab. "It's bigger," I whispered. "It's *growing*."

"What, baby?" Mom asked.

I shook my head. "Nothing," I mumbled. I knew she wouldn't believe me. I lowered my arm back to my side.

I shivered. How long would it take for the scab to get so big it covered my whole arm? My whole *body?*

The doctor has to help me, I thought.

Mom pulled my extra comforter out of the closet and spread it over me. "You're shaking," she said.

The doorbell rang. "That should be the doctor," Mom told me.

"He'll fix you right up," Dad promised as we waited.

My door opened and Mom stepped back in. "Honey, this is Dr. Brock. He's not your usual doctor—but he's filling in for Dr. Walker until Dr. Walker is back from vacation."

I hope he'll listen to me, I thought. If he doesn't . . .

Mom led the doctor into the room.

I stared up at him. Baggy long-sleeved shirt. Long green pants.

He leaned toward me. Peering at me through thick, thick glasses. His black eyes glittering.

"Noooo!" I yelled. "Get him away from me. He's the Bugman!"

14

~~~~~~

The Bugman! He followed me.

"It's the Bugman!" I shouted. "I have to get out of here!"

I threw off the comforter and scrambled out of bed. But before I got halfway to the door, Dad grabbed my by the shoulders.

Dad wouldn't let go. He turned me around to face the Bugman. I opened my mouth to scream again.

Wait. Wait. It isn't the Bugman.

The doctor wore the same thick glasses. But the doctor had curly blond hair. He smiled at me gently.

"Janet, this is Dr. Brock, Dr. Brock," my mother repeated over and over.

I nodded. "I'm sorry," I mumbled. I felt like such an idiot. I returned to the bed and sat down.

"It's okay," Dr. Brock answered. "Most people with high fevers have some strange thoughts."

Oh, no! He'll never believe me now. He'll never believe that the Bugman has done something horrible to me!

Dr. Brock did all the usual stuff. Made me cough while he listened with the stethoscope. Used a little light to check my eyes. Looked in my ears and throat.

"Nothing serious," he told my parents. "I'll give you a prescription for some antibiotics. Janet will be fine in no time."

"What about this scab?" I blurted out. I held up my arm.

Dr. Brock turned to me. He ran his fingers over the huge purple-black scab.

I have to at least try and get him to help me, I thought. "This happened when the Bugman spit at me. The spit was bright green. It landed right there." I pointed to the scab.

"I'll get you an ointment for that," Dr. Brock told me. He glanced at my parents. "If it doesn't start clearing up in a few days, let me know."

70

"Please listen. Mom, Dad, make him listen," I begged. "Break open the scab. There is this green stuff in it. *Green.* Like the juice the Bugman gave me to drink."

I scratched the scab with both hands, trying to show them the oily green mucus. "You can do tests on it!" I cried.

My parents each grabbed one hand. "Calm down, sweetie. Calm down," Mom pleaded.

"This medicine should take the fever down," Dr. Brock said. "It may make her very sleepy, but right now she needs a lot of rest."

"No!" I protested. No, I can't sleep. I have to do something. The scab was growing. The Bugman was after me. If I went to sleep now . . .

Dr. Brock handed me two tiny pills. Mom gave me the glass of ice water from my bedside table.

I tried to swallow the water without swallowing the pills—but they started to dissolve in my mouth. They tasted so bitter I swallowed them before I could stop myself.

"Bye, Janet," Dr. Brock said. "Call me if the fever doesn't break," he added to my mom.

"We'll let you sleep now," my dad said. "We'll be right downstairs if you need us."

Okay, I thought as my parents and Dr. Brock left the room. I'll wait for a while, then I'll sneak out.

I yawned. I felt so tired. So sleepy.

I stretched out on the bed. I'll close my eyes, I thought. Just for a minute. Just for a minute.

When I opened my eyes, I couldn't see anything. Blackness surrounded me.

"Mom," I called. My mouth felt dry and gritty. "Mom?" I tried again. No answer.

The bed felt so hard. And cold.

I squinted, trying to see through the darkness. Tiny dots of light came into focus. Hundreds of dots of light.

Stars, I realized. Those are stars!

I'm outside!

How did I get out here? Did I sleepwalk?

I tried to sit up—but I couldn't. I couldn't move.

What is going on? I thought. What's happening to me now?

I fought to lift my head, the muscles in my neck straining. Then I stared down at my body.

A low moan escaped from my throat. My body . . . I was buried in mud up to my neck.

How did I get out here?

Who did this to me?

"Mom!" I yelled. But my throat was too dry to make much sound. She would never hear me from all the way down here.

I struggled to sit up again. But the mud was packed tightly around me.

No, not just mud, I realized. A mix of mud and leaves and twigs that formed a shell around me.

No! Not a shell.

A *cocoon!*

15

I pulled my hands out of the muddy cocoon and started to pull the leaves and twigs off me. As I did, parts of a dream came back to me. I saw myself climbing out of bed—walking to this tree and working to build this cocoon. But it wasn't a dream. It was real. I made this cocoon because I'm turning into a bug.

The Bugman is turning me into a huge bug. I'll end up exactly like him.

"Noooo," I wailed. "No, I don't want to be a bug!" I had to stop him. Somehow I had to stop him.

I struggled to kick my feet and break through the shell. I could only get my toes to move a few inches.

I dug harder with my hands, tearing at the mud on my legs.

Hurry, hurry, hurry, I ordered myself. I didn't know how much time I had. How long would the transformation take? How long would I still be human?

I wriggled and kicked until my legs broke free.

Then I scrambled up. I was covered with leaves and twigs and grass and mud. I brushed off as much as I could. I touched my arms and legs searching for more of those horrible scabs. But the mud was too thick.

I tiptoed to the back door and opened it as quietly as I could. I didn't want Mom or Dad to see me like this. They wouldn't believe me. They would get the doctor back here in a second.

I didn't turn on the lights. I crept through the kitchen and down the stairs to the basement. I washed up at the big sink.

The scab on my arm was a little bigger. But I didn't see any other changes. At least not yet.

I put on clean clothes from the laundry basket and rolled the muddy ones into a little ball. I stuffed them behind the dryer. I'd figure out what to do with them later.

I had no time now. All that mattered was getting to the Bugman.

I reached the kitchen door. It swung open before I could grab the doorknob.

"Janet!" my mom exclaimed. "What are you doing down there? I went into your room to check on you and you were gone."

Oh, no! Now what am I going to do? I didn't have one second to waste.

"Um, I guess I was sleepwalking," I told her. "I'll just go back up to bed." I tried to rush past her.

"That happened when you were nine and had a fever," Mom answered. She followed right behind me. "I'll sit with you until you fall asleep."

I'm doomed. Doomed, I thought. There is no way out of this.

I had no choice. I followed Mom upstairs.

Tap. Tap. Tap.

Mom poked her head in the door. "You had a good sleep," she said. She hurried over and pressed her hand on my forehead. "And your fever is down."

"I feel fine," I answered. I swung my legs off the bed. I had to convince Mom to let me outside.

"Not so fast," she said. "You're going to spend the day in bed. But your friend Willow is downstairs if you feel well enough to see her."

"Willow? Yes! I want to see her. Please," I said in a rush.

"For a short visit," Mom answered. "You're not over this virus yet." She headed downstairs. A few minutes later Willow peeked into my room.

"Come inside and close the door," I ordered her. "I have something really important to tell you."

Willow rushed over and sat down on my bed. "Your mom said you were really sick," she said.

"The Bugman is doing something horrible to me," I began. "I think he's turning me into a bug. You've got to help me."

Willow tried to smile. But she looked worried.

"Oh—my mother must have told you I would say that," I said. "She thinks my fever made me delirious or something. But it didn't. And anyway I feel fine now."

I took a big breath and hurried on. "I went to the Bugman's house yesterday—"

"*What?*" Willow interrupted.

"I had to," I answered. "I had to try and find a way to stop him."

"Wait, wait. Slow down," Willow protested. "What happened after I saw you that day with the tarantula?"

"I went to Mr. Cooney's the next day. He wanted me to drink more of this green juice he makes—he's been giving it to me every day since I met him. I

77

wouldn't. I dropped the glass on the ground. All these bugs started drinking it—and getting bigger and bigger."

"But—" Willow began.

"Let me finish," I said. I could tell Willow was ready to interrupt again. I talked faster and faster so she wouldn't have a chance. I needed to tell her everything before my mom came back upstairs.

"Last night he caught me spying on him—and he ripped his face right off," I continued. "His human face was a mask. He really has the head of a giant fly or something."

"Whoa," Willow whispered. She hesitated. "Janet, don't get mad, okay? Couldn't your mom be right? Couldn't you have imagined the whole thing?"

"No way!"

Willow held up her hand. "Listen. When you're sick you can have some really weird dreams, even visions. I remember when I—"

"It wasn't a dream!" I insisted. *"Or* a vision. It wasn't.

"You've got to help me figure out a way to get back over to the Bugman's house. My mom will hardly let me out of her sight. But if I don't figure out what he's doing to me—I won't be able to stop him."

"Okay, okay," Willow said softly. "I believe you."

Willow thought for a minute. "I'll go for you," she

said. "It's the only way. We'd never be able to sneak you out past your mom."

"No. No, you can't go over there alone. It's too dangerous," I told her.

"I'll be careful. I'll look for evidence that he can turn people into bugs. And maybe I can get a sample of that juice," Willow said.

"I don't know," I said. "It's too scary. He really is a monster."

"Don't worry," Willow whispered. "I'll be careful. I'll go to his house right now. Don't worry. We'll find a way to stop the Bugman together."

"Thank you," I said. "Thank you so, so much. You're the best, Willow."

"I'll come back here as soon as I'm done," Willow promised. She jumped up and rushed out the door without looking back.

I climbed out of bed and stared down at the front yard. I watched Willow run out of the door and head toward Fear Street.

I rubbed my fingers over the scab on my arm. Bigger. Definitely bigger.

I watched Willow turn down Fear Street. Toward the Bugman's house.

Was she already too late?

16

I climbed back in bed and pulled my comforter up to my chin. Mom brought up some magazines, but I couldn't concentrate on reading. All I could think about was Willow.

I tried to picture every step she made—so I would know when to expect her back.

Okay. She left my room, walked down the stairs, said bye to my mom. Then put on her purple and yellow backpack, went out the front door, and ran down the street.

I could imagine everything Willow did—until she got to the Bugman's house. Then I couldn't come up with anything. I didn't know what would happen there.

And I couldn't do anything to help Willow. That was the worst.

I checked the clock. 11:14. Not even an hour since Willow left.

I asked Mom to bring the little TV from the kitchen upstairs. But even the wacko people on the talk shows couldn't hold my attention.

I checked the clock again. 1:00.

She should be back by now, I thought. I picked at the ragged skin around my thumbnail. She really should be back by now.

Maybe she had to wait for the Bugman to leave the room where his desk is. That could take a while.

Mom brought me up some lunch. I wasn't very hungry, but I ate some anyway. Then I tried to take a nap. But I couldn't fall asleep.

I rolled over onto my side and stared at my scab. Was it really bigger? Were there more of them? I couldn't tell anymore.

I looked at my alarm clock. Watching the seconds and minutes change. Waiting for Willow.

2:00. 3:00. 4:00. 5:00. No Willow.

Maybe I should call Carl and ask him to look for her. But the phone was downstairs. Mom might hear me.

Mom would think I was delirious again. I couldn't

risk her giving me another sleeping pill. I had to stay awake. I had to wait for Willow.

Dad came up to visit. I didn't feel like talking.

6:00. 7:00. 8:00. No Willow. And it would be dark soon.

I crawled out of bed and stared out the window. The street stood empty. What am I going to do if she doesn't come back?

9:00. 10:00. No Willow.

It was too dark to see anything out the window. I paced around my room. I felt too nervous to stay still.

Mom and Dad came in to say good night.

11:00. No Willow.

The Bugman has Willow!

Willow was trying to help me—and the Bugman got her. I knew it.

I'm sneaking out, I decided. I have to. I have to save Willow.

I pulled on jeans, sneakers, and a long-sleeved black T-shirt and started for my bedroom door. No. I couldn't risk going out the front way. I would have to walk right past Mom and Dad's bedroom—and one of them would hear me.

I opened my window and crawled out onto the garage roof. I slowly inched my way down to the edge and looked over. I grabbed the gutter and slid to the ground, holding on to the drainpipe.

I made it!

I took off for Fear Street. Please let me be in time, I thought. Please.

The Bugman's house stood dark and silent. I climbed over the back fence.

The garbage can. Where is it? I thought. I looked around. Then I saw something that made me gasp.

A piece of purple and yellow cloth rested on top of the Bugman's tombstone. It had to be Willow's. She always wore those colors.

I looked at the house. Still dark. I hurried over to the tombstone.

I grabbed the yellow and purple material. It's Willow's backpack, I realized.

Suddenly the ground rumbled and shook.

I fell onto the Bugman's tombstone.

What's happening? I thought. An earthquake?

Craaack!

The tombstone broke in half. The earth underneath it began to crumble.

A pit opened up. The two big pieces of granite started to slide into the pit.

I threw myself off the stone. Digging my fingers into the grass and weeds. Holding on, desperately clutching at the ground. Tearing at the dirt. Grabbing anything to keep from falling into the pit.

The earth bucked and shook. But I hung on—my legs dangling over the gaping pit.

Then the ground stopped shaking.

Still. Quiet. I crawled away from the pit—scraping my knees on stones and twigs.

Something sharp clamped around my ankle. It tore through the leg of my jeans.

I twisted around. "Noooo!" I shrieked.

The Bugman. He jerked on my ankle, pulling me down.

Down into his grave!

17

"**S**top!" I screamed. "Let me go!"

The Bugman tightened his grip on my foot and yanked it hard.

I couldn't hold on. I slid into the grave. Down. Down. Down.

The earth rumbled, closing in around me. I couldn't see. My mouth and nose filled with dirt.

I couldn't breathe. My lungs ached and burned.

Then I was falling. Falling through the air.

Thunk!

I landed at the bottom of the grave. I sat up, coughing and choking.

I heard a sound behind me. I jumped up and turned around fast. The Bugman stood there watching me.

A whimper escaped from my throat. For the first time I saw the Bugman's true form. I couldn't stop staring at him.

His back . . . his back was covered by a shiny purple-black shell. The same color as the scab on my arm!

His legs were as skinny as broom handles.

And he had four arms. Two arms the regular human size and shape. And two shorter, thinner arms growing out of the center of his chest.

Each arm ended in a sharp pincer. The Bugman clicked them open and shut as he studied me with his enormous eyes. *Click! Click! Click! Click!*

"Come with me," the Bugman ordered in his high voice. He grabbed my wrist in his pincer. Then he pulled me through a narrow dirt tunnel.

We entered a large chamber—bigger than the first—filled with a strange yellow glow.

Where is that light coming from? I knew we were still underground.

Lightning bugs! Lightning bugs are giving the light, I realized. They clung to the sides of the hollowed-out room. Thousands of them, blinking on and off in different rhythms.

"Hello, hello, my dears," the Bugman crooned. He

released my wrist and scuttled over to the wall. "My sweet darlings," he called to the lightning bugs.

"I told everyone about you!" I shouted. "They will come looking for me—so you better let me out of here right now!"

The Bugman gave a high, shrill shriek. He spun toward me. I felt his hot breath hit my face. It smelled like rotting lettuce.

Then I heard a sucking, slurping sound. He's going to spit on me again! I covered my face with my arms and backed away from him.

"Janet!"

I recognized the voice at once!

"Willow? Where are you?" I stared around the large room.

"I'm here. On the floor."

Then I saw her. Wrapped in a cocoon from her neck to her feet.

I dashed over to her and kneeled down next to her. "The Bugman got you, too! Are you okay?"

She looked past me and smiled. "See? I *told* you she would come, Father!"

18

~~~~

Father?

"No. No, Willow!" I cried. "The Bugman can't be your father. He must have given you something to make you believe that."

I grabbed the top of Willow's cocoon. "I'm tearing you out of there!" I yelled.

"Janet, don't!" Willow shouted. "You'll hurt me!"

The Bugman grabbed me by the back of my shirt and threw me against the wall. Then he came toward me. *Click! Click! Click! Click!*

"No, Father!" Willow exclaimed. "Don't hurt her! She's my friend. I want her for my friend."

The Bugman stared at me with his enormous black eyes. "I want you to be my Willow's friend, Janet. I won't hurt you—as long as you don't hurt Willow or the babies."

He really is her father, I realized. Willow tricked me. She planned to get me here all along!

"Why did you do this to me?" I yelled at Willow.

The Bugman began to hum. A high, whining sound.

How will I ever get out of here? What am I going to do? Mom and Dad don't know where I went. Maybe there's a way.

"I wanted you to be my friend," Willow said.

She sounded hurt. I couldn't believe it.

"You've got to listen to me. Please," Willow begged.

The Bugman pointed at her with one sharp pincer. Silently ordering me over to her.

I'll go along with them for a while, I decided. Until I can figure out what to do. I shuffled back over to Willow and sat down next to her cocoon.

"Okay. I'm listening. What?" I asked.

"I needed a friend. And I picked you," Willow answered. I noticed her green eyes glistening with tears.

"We *are* friends," I protested. I didn't want to

89

make Willow—or her father—upset again. Not until I found a way out of there.

"You don't understand," she said. "You can't really be my friend. Not the way you are. No one can."

I took a quick peek at the Bugman. He stood only a few feet behind me.

"Why not?" I asked.

"Because I'm only human part of the time. For two years I'm a girl. Then I go into a cocoon and spend two years as—"

"As a *bug?*" I interrupted. My stomach turned over.

"Yes. And it's so lonely. I make new friends. And then I lose them." Willow smiled up at me. "But now Father figured out a way to change you, too. Now we can be friends forever. Isn't that great?"

Great? She's nuts, I thought.

"I don't want to be a bug, Willow," I explained.

"Oh, you'll love it! You get to live in two worlds this way," Willow said. "You really feel part of the great circle of life. It's awesome!"

"But what about my family?" I asked. "I'll miss them."

"Father and I will be your family," Willow reassured me.

What could I say now? "But . . . but your father hates me. I destroyed his tombstone. I woke him from the dead."

Hmmm. Hmmm. Hmmm. The Bugman had started his humming again. But it sounded different. Lower. Not so piercing.

I glanced back at him. He rocked back and forth on his thin, thin legs, rubbing his pincers together. *Hmmm. Hmmm. Hmmm.*

The Bugman is laughing! I realized.

"What's so funny?" I asked.

"I was never dead," he answered in his high voice. "I was hibernating. A trick I learned from the seven-year locusts."

"But what about the tombstone?" I asked.

"Some boys put it there," the Bugman told me. "They became frightened of me once I began experimenting on myself. They didn't understand the thrill of transformation—of becoming half bug and half human."

The Bugman shook his head. "A group of them took me from my home and buried me in the yard," he continued. He began to click his pincers open and shut. "They thought I was dead. They put the tombstone on top of me."

He made his laughing-humming sound again. "But I wasn't dead. I was hibernating."

I swallowed hard. The Bugman could never be destroyed! I was trapped.

"See, Janet?" Willow said. "We'll be giving you a great new life. You'll live hundreds more years than most people."

"Thank you. I appreciate it, really," I told the Bugman. Then I turned my gaze to Willow. "But please choose someone else. I know it doesn't make sense to you, but I want to stay human."

"It's too late for that," the Bugman said. "The process has already begun."

My heart pounded so loud I could hardly hear him. "What?" I cried.

The Bugman scurried over to the dirt wall behind Willow. "Excuse me, babies," he said. He gently shooed some of the fireflies away.

Now I could see a small hole dug into the wall. A pitcher sat inside it. The same pitcher the Bugman used to serve the green juice.

Then I understood. "I was right!" I yelled. I jumped to my feet. "That juice you kept giving me—and the health shake Willow made—it's already started turning me into a bug."

"Yes," the Bugman answered. He picked up the pitcher and started toward me. "Now, have some more."

"No!" I shouted.

"Please, Janet. Be reasonable," the Bugman said.

"Never! Let me out of here!"

"Very well," the Bugman said firmly. "Babies! Do your work!"

19

Hundreds of bugs swarmed through the earth and came toward me. Beetles. Ants. Centipedes.

Something soft brushed against my face. Soft and sticky. I looked up. "No," I whispered.

A fat gray spider hung on a shiny thread in front of my nose. Another spider slithered down. Faster and faster, they dropped their threads around me.

I slashed my hand across the threads, and the spiders fell to the ground. More spiders slid down to take their place.

My ankles started to itch and burn. I stared down.

The cuffs of my jeans bulged as the army of bugs shoved their way inside.

I shook one leg, then the other. Bugs tumbled back onto the ground. But more kept coming.

Then I heard buzzing—getting louder and louder. I squeezed my eyes shut. I didn't want to see the wasps and bees arrive.

"Willow!" I screamed. "Help me! Please!"

Bugs flew into my mouth. I choked, coughing and spitting.

"It will be okay, Janet," Willow called. "Don't fight it. Let them build the cocoon. It's the final stage."

Cocoon? They're building a cocoon?

I opened my eyes. Every inch of my body was covered with bugs.

I tried to knock them off. But I couldn't. My arms were pinned to my sides.

The spiders are spinning webs around me, I realized. That's why I can't move.

A row of ants climbed onto my face. Each carried tiny twigs and pieces of leaves. They stuck to my skin.

The bees and wasps dive-bombed me. Dropping more leaves and bits of wax and honey.

Then all the insects turned and swarmed away from me. Burrowing into the soil. Climbing back into the ceiling. Flying out the tunnel.

"It's almost over," Willow called.

Almost?

The earth moved again. And rows and rows of thick yellow slugs burst through. They slithered toward me, and then crept up my body.

Their cold slime trails sealed the cocoon even more tightly.

I couldn't move at all.

The Bugman's babies had finished their work. They slid off me and disappeared.

"Time to sleep now," the Bugman announced in a singsong voice. He scurried over to Willow with the pitcher of green juice. He bent down and poured some into her mouth.

"See you when we wake up, Janet!" Willow cried. "Just think of this as a slumber party—with our cocoons as sleeping bags."

"Willow, no. Tell your father you changed your mind," I pleaded.

But she didn't answer.

The Bugman kissed Willow on the forehead. "Good night, Princess," he said.

"Good night, Father," she said. The Bugman placed a loose hood over her head. It looked as if it were made of spiderwebs.

Then the Bugman turned to me.

"No," I begged. "Please don't do this. Please. I

want to go home to my family. I want to stay human."

The Bugman shook his head. "It will all be over soon," he said. He pressed the pitcher of juice against my lips.

20

I twisted my head back and forth violently. I couldn't drink that juice.

The Bugman uttered a high, angry whine. He trapped my head between two of his pincers and forced the spout of the pitcher between my lips.

"Drink!" he ordered.

I clenched my teeth. Clenched them until my jaws ached.

Then the Bugman clamped my nose closed with one pincer. I couldn't breathe.

My chest started to burn. But I didn't open my

mouth. My heart thudded harder and harder. But I kept my teeth locked together.

Air, I thought. I need air.

Tiny red dots burst in front of my eyes.

I had to have air.

I opened my mouth and sucked in a big breath.

I tried to slam my teeth shut again. Too slow. The Bugman tilted back my head and poured the green juice into my mouth.

No! I won't drink it, I thought.

I spit it out—aiming for the Bugman's black eyes.

He squealed in pain. Got him!

The Bugman dropped the pitcher onto the ground and stumbled away from me. He scrubbed at his eyes with all four pincers.

"You are not worthy of being my daughter's friend!" the Bugman screamed. His antennae whipped back and forth. Green drool dripped from his mouth. He began snapping all four pincers open and closed.

I wiggled and squirmed, trying to break free of the cocoon. But the webbing was too tight. My arms stayed glued to my sides. And my feet were locked together.

"I was going to give you a beautiful life—but you're not worthy!" the Bugman shrieked. "Now you must be *exterminated!*"

21

~~~

The Bugman charged at me.

I threw my weight forward—and slammed into him. We both fell.

I rolled over and over, still trapped in my tight cocoon. Then I thudded to a stop against the crumbly dirt wall.

The Bugman gave a shrill squeal.

He's coming after me, I thought. And I can't even stand up.

I twisted my neck around. Where is he?

Then I saw him. He lay flat on his big purple-black shell. All four arms and his skinny legs waved wildly in the air.

He can't stand up! I knocked him over. He landed on his back—and he can't flip himself back over.

"Babies!" the Bugman cried. "Babies, help me. Help me."

All the bugs swarmed back up from the floor and walls and ceiling. Thousands of them. They crawled over the Bugman.

What if they are strong enough to help him up? I had to get out of the cocoon. Fast.

I rolled back and forth, struggling to break free of the webbing. But the cocoon didn't feel any looser.

I grabbed hold of the webbing under my chin the only way I could. With my teeth.

I gave it a yank—and a piece ripped off. I spit it out and bit into another section, the leaves and twigs crunching in my mouth. Gross!

I tore away as much of the webbing as I could reach. The cocoon felt looser now, and I could move one arm a little.

I glanced over at the Bugman. I couldn't see him at all. The insects covered him completely.

Hurry, I ordered myself. If his babies flip him right side up, you're dead.

I worked my arm back and forth until it burst free. I tore at the cocoon until I could use my other arm, too. Faster, faster, I thought.

I ripped a big piece of webbing off my legs and then kicked my way out of the bottom of the cocoon. I struggled to my feet and raced down the narrow tunnel.

I could still hear the Bugman screaming. Then I heard another voice. Willow's.

"Janet," Willow called. "Don't go! Don't you want to be my friend?"

I didn't answer. There is nothing I can do for her, I told myself. The tunnel split in two directions. One seemed to run uphill. I followed it, the dirt making me choke and cough.

The tunnel hit a dead end. I dug frantically, bringing down clumps of dirt on my head. Then I felt a cool breeze on my face—and saw the stars shining above me.

As I hauled myself through the hole I heard Willow's voice echo through the tunnel behind me. "Janet. Don't go. Stay. Don't you want to be my friend?"

Epilogue

*W*hap!

"Oww!" My back stung like crazy. I sat up and grabbed the beach towel out of Carl Beemer's hands. "You jerk!" I yelled.

Carl laughed and cannonballed into the pool, sending a tidal wave onto my notebook. He came up smirking.

"Jerk," I muttered again. Megan would be back tomorrow. And Anita and Sara would be home on Friday. I couldn't wait.

Carl swam over and rested his arms on the edge of

the pool. I held up my sopping notebook. "You got water all over my story," I snapped.

"You should change it anyway," Carl answered. I noticed he didn't bother to apologize. Typical.

"I think you should make me the hero," Carl continued. "I could run into the Bugman's lair and rescue you and Willow and get my picture in the paper."

"Yeah, right," I said. "As if you would do something that brave."

I smoothed the wrinkly pages of the notebook. "I just finished the end."

"Let's hear it," Carl said.

" 'Nobody knew what happened to the Bugman or Willow after that,' " I read. " 'They disappeared— and only the Bugman's big purple-black shell was ever found.

" 'But what I cared about was that I was still *me*. Not a bug. Just a girl. A *human* girl. The End.' "

Carl snorted. He sounds like a hog when he does that. "Not bad," he admitted. "You might win that story contest in the paper. Since *I* didn't bother to write one myself."

He splashed some water in my face. "Yeah. It took a wild imagination to come up with a wacko story like that," Carl added. "What are you going to call it anyway?"

104

I thought for a minute. " 'The Bugman Lives!' " I announced.

I headed for home, my hair still wet from the pool. A beautiful purple and yellow butterfly fluttered around my head.

"Hey, I was hoping you'd come by the pool," I said.

The butterfly took off and landed near the top of the maple tree in the Hasslers' yard.

I rubbed my hands together. Sticky green mucus began oozing across my palms.

"I'll meet you up there," I called.

Slurp, slurp, slurp. I climbed straight up the trunk of the maple tree. This green stuff works better than suction cups, I thought.

The purple and yellow butterfly flew over and sat on my nose. I grinned at it. "I'm glad we're friends," I said. "I'd hate to spend the *whole* day with Carl."

The butterfly beat its wings together.

"I never could have climbed this high before I met you," I told the butterfly. "You were right, Willow. Some parts of being a bug *can* be awesome."

Are you ready for another walk
down Fear Street?
Turn the page for a terrifying
sneak preview.

R·L·STINE'S
GHOSTS of FEAR STREET® #11

THE BOY WHO ATE
FEAR STREET

Coming mid-August 1996

"**H**elp!" I cried, leaping up from my chair. "My mouth is on fire!"

Mrs. Sullivan handed me a glass of milk. I gulped it down. Then I reached over and grabbed Lissa's glass of milk. I gulped that down too.

The burning feeling spread across my lips and down my throat. Even my chest felt scorched, and my tongue began to swell.

I grabbed every glass of milk on the table and gulped it down. Then I snatched the milk container from the kitchen counter and chugged that.

"Are you okay, dear?" Aunt Sylvie asked, patting me on the back.

"What . . . did . . . you . . . put . . . in . . . my . . . pudding?" I sputtered, jerking away from her.

"Aunt Sylvie didn't put anything in your rice pudding," Lissa said. "You probably just swallowed wrong."

The Sullivans and Kevin nodded in agreement, but Aunt Sylvie tapped the side of her forehead with her index finger. "Hmmmm, let me think. Let me think," she repeated over and over again.

While Aunt Sylvie tried to remember, I poked around the top layer of rice pudding with my spoon.

I found rice. I found pudding.

Nothing else.

I poked around some more.

Aha! At the bottom of the bowl I found what I was looking for. Little dark flakes. So little that I thought they were specks of cinnamon at first.

"What's *this?*" I asked Aunt Sylvie, pointing a shaky finger into my bowl.

"Great Uncle Henry!" Aunt Sylvie exclaimed.

"Huh?"

"Now I remember! While I was making the rice pudding, the spirit of Uncle Henry visited for a chat," Aunt Sylvie began to explain. "And he suggested that I use the new spice I brought back from the Orient."

Aunt Sylvie held up a bottle of flakes. "I enjoyed speaking to Uncle Henry." She sighed. "We've spoken so little since he died."

"Aunt Sylvie," Mrs. Sullivan chided, "you're going to scare the children."

"Oh, nonsense!" Aunt Sylvie chuckled. "The children know what an odd creature I am!"

Everyone at the table laughed. Everyone but me.

"I'm sorry the spice burned your tongue," Aunt Sylvie said, turning to me. "It's supposed to be tangy—not hot."

"Maybe it turned rotten," I murmured.

Aunt Sylvie reached over for my bowl of rice pudding. She lifted it to her nose and sniffed. "It smells okay, but I bet you're right. It probably has spoiled. I'm going to throw it out—right now."

"Aren't you going to taste it first?" I asked. "Maybe it's not spoiled. Maybe it was just too spicy for me."

"Taste it?" Aunt Sylvie gasped. "Oh, no! *I'm* not going to taste it."

"What?" I shouted. Why aren't you going to taste it?" I leaped up from my chair.

Aunt Sylvie didn't reply.

She headed toward the sink and emptied the jar of flakes down the drain.

"Why didn't you taste it?" I demanded.

"Oh, those flakes are much too strong for me!" Aunt Sylvie smiled. "I don't care for tangy food myself. Now—who would like some vanilla ice cream? I bet you would, Sam. Right?"

Everyone ate the ice cream, except me. Those black specks in the ice cream were probably vanilla beans—but I wasn't taking any chances.

After dinner, Kevin, Lissa, and I played Kevin's LaserBlast video game. I usually win—but not this time. My stomach was upset, and I felt weird. Kind of hot all over.

"See you guys tomorrow," I told Kevin and Lissa when it was time to leave.

"Great!" Kevin walked me to the front door. "Aunt Sylvie has some more awesome things you've got to see!"

"And maybe she'll let us play with her snake, Shirley!" Lissa called from the den.

I didn't think I wanted to see any more of Aunt Sylvie's things—or play with Shirley. I knew for sure that I didn't want to eat any more of her cooking.

When I reached home, my stomach was still upset so I went right up to bed. I snuggled under my blanket, tucked it under my chin, and fell asleep instantly.

I don't know how much later it was when I woke

up. But all the lights were out, and Mom and Dad were in bed.

I made my way down the dark hall, down the steps, and into the kitchen. My stomach felt much better—back to normal. Now I was hungry. I knew just what I wanted—my favorite sandwich, mayonnaise on white bread.

A full moon hung in the sky. It lit the kitchen with a warm glow. *I'd better not put the light on,* I thought as I searched the kitchen counter for the bread. *I don't want to wake Mom or Dad.*

After I found the bread, I hunted for a new jar of mayonnaise in the pantry—I finished the old jar at lunch. I eat a lot of mayonnaise—about a jar a week. I can't help it. I really love the stuff!

I stifled a yawn, then, half asleep, I made my sandwich. When it was ready, I sunk my teeth in for a really big bite.

Delicious.

Plain old white food—without a single one of Aunt Sylvie's spices from around the world.

I took another bite. And another. And another.

I needed something to drink.

I opened the refrigerator and grabbed a bottle of Sprite.

The light from the refrigerator fell on the kitchen counter.

On my half-eaten sandwich.

I stared at the sandwich.

Something was wrong with it. Very wrong.

I rubbed my eyes and focused. I stared at it again, harder this time. Something still didn't seem right.

I lowered my face to the counter.

I squinted at the sandwich—and screamed.

Sponges! Not bread!

I made a sandwich with two moldy green sponges. And I ate it. And it tasted good.

How could I have made a sponge sandwich? How could I have eaten it? HOW?

The room began to spin. I grabbed hold of the kitchen counter to steady myself.

That's when I saw the yellow ooze seeping out from my sponge sandwich.

"Oh, no," I moaned. *What did I spread inside those slices?*

I didn't want to look, but I had to.

I lifted the top sponge. My hand shook.

The yellow ooze ran off the sponge and dripped along the counter, and my stomach lurched.

I dipped my finger into it. Sniffed it.

It smelled lemony. Soapy.

Lemon-fresh dish detergent.

I just ate a soap-and-sponge sandwich. And I liked it.

What is wrong with me? How could I have eaten that?

I quickly tossed the sponges into the trash and ran upstairs to my bedroom. I dove under the covers and stared out my bedroom window at the dark, cloudless sky.

I asked myself over and over again, *How could I have eaten that? How? How? How?*

And then the answer came to me.

I was sleepwalking. That had to be it. I dreamed that I was hungry, and I sleepwalked into the kitchen and made myself a sandwich.

The light from the refrigerator woke me up—and that's when I realized what I was doing.

It really did make sense. Mom says Dad walks in his sleep all the time.

I felt better.

I leaned back against my pillow, closed my eyes, and fell asleep.

"Sam! Time to get up!" Mom called up the stairs. "Time for breakfast!"

I pulled on my favorite navy blue T-shirt and my favorite jeans—the ones with the rip in the knee. I slipped on my sneakers and ran downstairs without tying the laces. Mom always yells at me for that. She says one day I'm going to trip and break my neck. Mothers say that kind of stuff to their kids.

I sat down at the kitchen table and took a big swallow of milk. "YUCK!"

"What's wrong, Sam?" Dad asked.

"The milk is sour!" I grumbled. "It's disgusting."

"It must be past the expiration date," Mom said. "And I just bought it yesterday. I'm going to bring it back to the grocery store and lodge a complaint." She rummaged through the garbage for the empty container.

She took the container from the trash. Then she lifted out the two green sponges. The two half-eaten green sponges.

I held my breath as she studied them.

No way was I going to admit I ate a sponge sandwich last night—even if I did do it in my sleep.

"Hey, Mom!" I tried to steal Mom's attention. "Aren't you going to check the expiration date on the milk?"

My plan didn't work.

Mom continued to stare at the sponges.

"Mom! I'm starving! What's for breakfast? I'm going to be late for school."

That worked.

She tossed the sponges back into the garbage. "How about some Cream of Wheat?" she asked. A smile formed on her lips. Mom knows that's my all-time favorite breakfast.

I nodded eagerly. Sometimes I eat two bowls of Cream of Wheat a day—one in the morning and one when I come home from school.

Mom set one bowl in front of me and one in front of Dad. Dad likes Cream of Wheat almost as much as I do.

White puffs of steam floated up from my cereal bowl. Ahhhh, I thought, Cream of Wheat—so nice, so white.

I couldn't wait to eat it. I really was starving.

I dipped my spoon into the bowl.

I slipped the spoon into my mouth.

The Cream of Wheat slid off onto my tongue—and my jaw dropped open in horror.

"Dad!" I screamed. "Don't eat the Cream of Wheat! *DON'T!*"

About R. L. Stine

R. L. Stine, the creator of *Ghosts of Fear Street*, has written almost 100 scary novels for kids. The *Ghosts of Fear Street* series, like the *Fear Street* series, takes place in Shadyside and centers on the scary events that happen to people who live there.

When he isn't writing, R. L. Stine likes to play pinball on his very own pinball machine, and explore New York City with his wife, Jane, and fifteen-year-old son, Matt.